Josie Smith

in hospital

MAGDALEN NABB

Josie Smith

in hospital

Illustrated by Pirkko Vainio

CollinsChildren'sBooks
An Imprint of HarperCollinsPublishers

First published in Great Britain by Collins 1993
Collins is an imprint of
HarperCollins*Publishers* Ltd,
77-85 Fulham Palace Road,
Hammersmith, London W6 8JB

The HarperCollins website address is
www.**fire**and**water**.com

7 9 11 13 15 14 12 10 8

Text copyright © Magdalen Nabb 1993
Illustrations copyright © Pirkko Vainio 1993

The author and illustrator assert the moral right to be
identified as the author and illustrator of the work.

ISBN 0 00 674720 5

Printed and bound in Great Britain by
Caledonian International Book Manufacturing Ltd,
Glasgow G64

Contents

For my sister Julia,
who wanted to be a nurse
when she grew up, and did

JOSIE SMITH'S
HORRIBLE DAY

On Saturday afternoon it was raining and
Josie Smith was fed up. She climbed onto
the big chair near the front window and
leant on her elbows to watch. The street
was dark and wet and nobody went past.
The raindrops that tried to trickle down the
glass got blown sideways by the wind. When
Josie Smith tried to follow one with her finger
it always got flattened and bumped into
another drop and disappeared. Josie Smith
hated the wind. It made a whiny, fed-up
noise that went on and on, just like Eileen
next door when she cried. Eileen was Josie
Smith's best friend and she was always
crying to get her own way. She was spoilt,
Josie's mum said.

Josie Smith leant her forehead against the window and sniffed. It smelt cold and dirty like the rain. Josie Smith climbed down from the big chair and said, "I'm fed up."

"Well, get something to do," said Josie's mum. She switched the light on and started polishing the sideboard.

"Can I have a new crayoning book?" Josie Smith said.

"No," said Josie's mum, "you can finish the one you've got."

"I have finished it," said Josie Smith. "I finished crayoning it ages ago and you promised I could have a new one if I crayoned nicely inside the lines."

"Don't pester," said Josie's mum. "You can have one next Saturday."

"You said that last Saturday!" shouted Josie Smith. "You said!"

"Don't you shout at me, young lady," said Josie's mum. She was really cross but Josie Smith didn't care, she was so fed up. She started crying.

"I never have anything! Eileen's always having things and I never have anything!"

"Eileen's spoilt," said Josie's mum. "I've told you before."

"I don't care," shouted Josie Smith. "I want to be spoilt. I want to be like Eileen and have everything I want."

"Go and live at Eileen's then," said Josie's mum, "and see how you like it. Go and learn to be spoilt and whine all the time and see how it suits you. Now, that's enough! Stop crying and say you're sorry."

But Josie Smith didn't stop crying. She didn't say she was sorry either. She pulled her slippers off and slammed them down in the kitchen and put her wellingtons on.

"Where do you think you're going?" said Josie's mum.

"Eileen's," said Josie Smith.

She waited to see if her mum would say she couldn't, but her mum didn't say anything. She just carried on polishing and looking cross. Josie Smith hung her raincoat over her head and went next door to Eileen's.

It was Eileen's mum who opened the door.

"I'm not playing!" Eileen shouted from behind her. But Eileen's mum said, "Come in."

Josie Smith went in and took her wellingtons off. Eileen was sitting on the carpet, dressing her doll. Josie Smith hadn't brought her doll so she sat down next to Eileen to help.

"Here's her bonnet," said Josie Smith.

Eileen snatched it and said, "I never said you could touch it. And anyway, I'm not playing with you today, I'm playing with Dora Whittacker."

Josie Smith didn't know who Dora

Whittacker was so she didn't say anything. She pulled her socks up and then sat still and watched Eileen dress her doll. The baby was crying in the kitchen.

"Eileen!" shouted Eileen's mum. "Get your coat on, we're going."

Eileen stood up and held her doll tight to her chest and said, "We're going to Mrs Whittacker's and Dora Whittacker's going to be there and she's older than me and I'm playing with her. And she's got nail varnish and we're going to put some on and it's pink."

Eileen's mum came in and said, "Get a move on. You as well, Josie. Get your coat on if you want to come."

"I'm playing with Dora Whittacker," Eileen said.

"You can all play together," said Eileen's mum.

Josie Smith didn't want to go. But she didn't want to go home either. She thought about the pink nail varnish and she put her raincoat and wellingtons on.

When they set off the baby was still

crying, but when it heard the rain pattering on the pram cover and hood it opened its eyes very wide and stopped. Then it fell asleep. Josie Smith and Eileen took turns at pushing the pram. Eileen always pushed for longer because it was her baby. The wheels left long lines on the dirty wet pavement. Eileen said, "When we go into hospital to have our tonsils out I'm having a special present and it's a secret."

"So am I," said Josie Smith, but she said it with her eyes a bit shut because it might be a lie. She didn't know if everybody got a present for going into hospital.

"We're here," said Eileen's mum, and they stopped.

Mrs Whittacker's house was very big and black with a lot of chimneys. Josie Smith was frightened of it but she wanted to see inside. There was a long passage where they left the pram, and Eileen's mum hung her coat up with a lot of other coats where there was a mirror. Josie Smith didn't like the smell and there was a big door with frightening coloured glass in it.

Mrs Whittacker had a white face and red lipstick. She didn't smile. She said, "You can take your coats off in the playroom." Then she went away with Eileen's mum.

The playroom was high and dark. There was an old lumpy settee in the middle and a lot of scratched chairs and there were broken toys and old dressing-up things everywhere, even on the floor and the table. Josie Smith and Eileen stood there near the door and waited.

"I'm not playing," a girl's voice said, "I've got a headache." But they couldn't see anybody.

Josie Smith and Eileen waited.

"You'll have to read a comic or something until I feel better." But they still didn't see anybody. Then a hand came over the back of the lumpy settee. A hand with bitten nails that had flecks of red nail varnish on them. Josie Smith and Eileen went round to the front of the settee. Dora Whittacker was lying on it with a pile of comics on the floor beside her. She had tiny eyes and long bony legs and she was a lot bigger than Josie Smith and Eileen.

They had to sit down without making a noise and pretend to read comics. They couldn't really read them because they couldn't see. There was a tall dark window with the rain trickling down it, but the long curtains were almost closed and anyway there was only a wet black wall outside it. Dora Whittacker wouldn't have the light on because she had a headache. Josie Smith felt frightened. She was frightened of the tall dark window and the smell of the playroom. She was frightened of Dora Whittacker's tiny eyes looking at her. She sat near Eileen on a hard chair and her chest went bam bam bam and she pretended to read her comic. Then Dora Whittacker said, "I'm better now," and switched the light on. She made them sit at the table that was covered in ripped books and plastic handbags and dolls' clothes and broken crayons and she made them listen to a story that she read out of a book. The book had pictures but she wouldn't show them until the end and then she showed them all.

"Now we can do our nails," Dora Whittacker said, and she opened a pale blue plastic handbag and took out a lot of bottles of nail varnish. They were all different colours. Some of the bottles were nearly empty and some of them wouldn't open. Dora Whittacker painted white nail varnish over the bits of red on her nails. Josie Smith and Eileen chose pink. The nail varnish was sticky and had lumps in it, but Josie Smith liked the smell of it and she forgot to feel

frightened because she was having a good time.

When they'd finished their nails and were waving their hands about to dry the nail varnish, Josie Smith said to Dora Whittacker, "Will your mum let you keep it on?"

"I haven't got a mum," Dora Whittacker said. "She ran away because she didn't want me."

"Why is Mrs Whittacker not your mum?" asked Josie Smith.

"Because she's my aunty, stupid. Sometimes I live here and sometimes I live with my dad but he doesn't really want me. Nobody can cope with me."

Josie Smith didn't say anything. Dora Whittacker didn't cry because she hadn't got a mum. Josie Smith wished she could run home and see if her mum was still there, but she couldn't because she didn't know the way. Dora Whittacker said, "I can do anything I want, anyway," and just to show them she got on the settee with her shoes on and started jumping up and down on it and screaming. Nobody came in to say Be quiet. Then Josie Smith and Eileen climbed up on the settee and they jumped up and down too and screamed as loud as they could. And even though Josie Smith's wellingtons and Eileen's shoes were wet and filthy, nobody came and stopped them or said Be quiet. When they were hot and red and tired out with screaming, Dora Whittacker said, "Now we're playing hospitals," and she whispered in Eileen's ear.

Eileen said to Josie Smith, "You've got to be in hospital and have your tonsils out and I'm the nurse and Dora Whittacker's the doctor. You've got to lie down with a blanket on and shut your eyes."

"I don't want to," Josie Smith said.

"Well, you've got to," Dora Whittacker said, "or else you're not playing and I'll tell over you for jumping on the settee in your wellingtons."

It wasn't fair because they'd all jumped on the settee. But only Josie Smith had wellingtons on so perhaps that was different. Josie Smith lay down on the settee and closed her eyes. Somebody put a doll's blanket on her near her face and she didn't like it because it smelled sickly.

Dora Whittacker said, "You've got to stay there with your eyes shut until we say you can get up."

Josie Smith stayed there with her eyes shut. She heard them whispering for a long time and then she heard Eileen giggling. Then some more whispering. Then it was quiet. Josie Smith waited a long time and then she opened her eyes just a bit to peep. She couldn't see anything. Somebody had turned the light off. She opened her eyes wider and there was nobody there. She pushed the smelly blanket away from her and sat up. The rain was still trickling down the tall dark window, the comics and toys were still all over the place and the bottles of nail varnish were still on the table. But Dora Whittacker and Eileen had gone.

At first, Josie Smith thought they were hiding. She thought they had pretended to play hospitals just to make her be on at hide and seek. She started looking. She looked behind the settee and in all the corners and under the table but Dora Whittacker and Eileen weren't there. She looked behind an armchair and inside a tall brown cupboard that creaked when she opened it. The cupboard was full of broken toys and old children's shoes but there was room to hide in it. Dora Whittacker and Eileen weren't there. Josie Smith stood in the middle of the big playroom and wondered what to do. She thought they might be hiding behind the half-drawn curtains but she was too frightened of the dark rainy window to go near it. She wondered where Eileen's mum was, and she wished she could go home. Then she heard somebody playing the piano in another room. On her tiptoes she went to the playroom door and opened it. The piano noise got louder. Then it stopped. A door with a fat round doorknob opened and Josie Smith saw a light on. Dora Whittacker and Eileen looked out from behind the door. "We're not playing with you," Dora Whittacker said, "because you're ugly." And

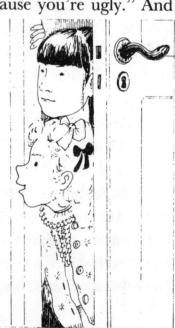

they went back in and slammed the door. The piano music started again. Eileen didn't know how to play the piano so it must be Dora Whittacker playing. Josie Smith stood still outside the door. Perhaps if she waited Eileen's mum would come.

Eileen's mum didn't come.

The piano music stopped and Dora Whittacker and Eileen opened the door again.

"You've got to go home," Dora Whittacker said.

Eileen laughed and then she said, "We've told over you for jumping on the settee with your wellingtons on and Mrs Whittacker says you've got to go home right away."

"And if you don't," Dora Whittacker said, "I'll thump you."

They went back in and slammed the door. Josie Smith heard them laughing. She ran back in the playroom and put her raincoat on and her chest was going bam bam bam because she was frightened of Dora Whittacker thumping her. She ran out of the playroom but she didn't know her way out of the house. She didn't want to go through the door with the frightening dark coloured glass in it so she ran along the passage the other way and through an ordinary door. She ran through a big empty kitchen and another door and a room with a lot of shelves and boxes and boots and a washing machine. Josie Smith stopped. There was a window, and through the window she could see a yard. Josie Smith found a cream painted door with a big key in it and she turned the key and got out into the yard. It was raining hard. The walls were black and dripping and rainwater was running in little rivers down the sloping yard towards some steps and a gate. Josie Smith went splashing down the steps and out through the gate and ran as fast as she could along the dirt road away from Mrs Whittacker's frightening house. When she couldn't run any more she stopped. She was out of breath and her chest hurt and her hands and face were wet.

"A-her! A-her! A-her!" panted Josie

Smith and she held her burning chest. When she stopped being out of breath she put her hood up and fastened her raincoat properly. Then she pulled her socks up because they'd rolled down under her feet inside her wellingtons. Her feet were cold. Her hands and face were cold as well.

"I'm going home," she said out loud. Then she looked around her. There was a dirt road behind her that went back to Mrs Whittacker's frightening house. In front of her there was some long wet grass and some stone steps down to a garden with bushes and puddles in it and a fence round it. After the fence there were wet fields and then more wet fields and then some small red houses miles and miles away. Josie Smith was lost.

"What am I going to do?" she whispered, standing still in the rain and trying not to cry.

A brown dog came trotting up the dirt road. He didn't sniff about or look at anything as he came so he must have been in a hurry to get somewhere, but Josie

Smith called to him to stop. The dog looked at her and thought for a minute and then he came up to her, wagging his tail. He was soaking wet. Josie Smith let him sniff her cold hand and said, "If you know a way out of this dirt road without going back past Mrs Whittacker's, I could come with you. I'm lost."

The dog sat down and looked at her hard.

"When I got lost at the seaside," Josie Smith told him, "a dog found me. He brought my mum and my gran."

The dog put his head on one side and looked at Josie Smith. Then he made a little whiny noise in his throat.

"I haven't got any bones," Josie Smith said, "but I've got some dolly mixtures in my pocket from this morning. There's not many but you can have one."

The dog looked hard at the crumpled paper bag that Josie Smith fished out of her pocket. She held out two dolly mixtures on the palm of her hand and said, "You can choose which one you like best."

The brown dog put his wet nose on Josie Smith's hand and sniffed. But he didn't choose. He just went "Glup!" and the dolly mixtures disappeared. Then he stood up and shook himself hard, showering rain everywhere. Josie Smith didn't care because she was wet already. They set off together down the dirt road. "I don't want to go past Mrs Whittacker's," Josie Smith said.

But they didn't go back that far. Between two high black houses there was a narrow path just wide enough for one person or one dog. Josie Smith followed the wet brown dog along the narrow path and came out at the front of the houses into a street. The dog started to run.

"Wait!" shouted Josie Smith. "Wait! This is not my street. I'm still lost!"

The dog turned round and came back for her. He sniffed at her and then set off again with Josie Smith running after him as fast as her wellingtons would go. They ran round one corner and then round another corner and then it stopped raining and the sun came out. A big blue space appeared in the sky. Josie Smith cheered up and ran even faster. Then the dog stopped.

Josie Smith stopped behind him. "A-her! A-her! A-her!" she went. "What have you stopped for? That's not my house."

But it was somebody's house. The door opened and a big rough boy came out. He looked at the brown dog and said, "Where've you been?"

The brown dog sat down and thumped his tail on the pavement and looked back at Josie Smith to show the boy that he'd brought something.

The rough boy looked at Josie Smith and showed her his fist.

"You'd better not steal my dog!"

Josie Smith was too frightened to say anything. She didn't even dare run away, in case he chased after her. The boy got hold of the dog by its collar.

"Somebody stole him once," he said, "and I set the police on them and then I thumped them."

Josie Smith looked at the boy's big dirty fists and her chest was going bam bam bam.

"Well?" shouted the boy. "Clear off, can't you?"

"I can't," Josie Smith said in a tiny voice, "I'm lost."

She tried as hard as she could not to cry but a few tears squeezed out anyway and she felt sick. She poked her hand in her raincoat pocket to see if there was a handkerchief. The brown dog came and sat

down in front of her, waiting for a dolly mixture. There was no handkerchief so Josie Smith got the bag of dolly mixtures out. The brown dog thumped his tail. She only gave him one this time.

The big boy said, "What's that?"

"A dolly mixture," said Josie Smith. "Don't thump me."

"You shouldn't give dogs toffees," said the big boy. "They get worms. You can give them to me."

Josie Smith held out the crumpled bag

and the boy took it off her. He poured all the dolly mixtures into his mouth at once and threw the bag in the road. Then he looked at Josie Smith and said, "You're not lost. I've seen you before playing with Gary Grimes. You live across from Mrs Chadwick's shop. What's your name?"

"Josie Smith," said Josie Smith.

"You great soft thing," said the big boy. "My mum goes to your house when she gets a frock sewn. It's only round the corner. You're daft, you!"

"I don't know which corner it is," said Josie Smith. She didn't feel as frightened of the big boy as she did before because his mum came to her mum to have her frocks sewn.

"Have you got any more toffees?" the big boy said.

"No," said Josie Smith.

"Well, I'll take you home if you want," he said, "only first you've got to play a game because I play with Mick Entwistle and he hasn't come out. It's cops and robbers. You have to go round that corner

29

and hide in the gateway where there's a step down until you hear me blow this whistle. Then you run for it and I catch you."

Josie Smith went and hid in the gateway where there was a step down.

"Count to a hundred!" shouted the big boy's voice. Josie Smith started counting but before she even got to twenty the whistle blew and she started to run. The big boy and the dog ran after her and the boy caught her.

"Are you taking me home now?" asked Josie Smith.

"Game's not finished," said the big boy. "Stand with your back to that lamp post."

Josie Smith stood. The boy got some dirty string from his pocket and tied Josie Smith's hands together behind the lamp post.

"Now you're caught," the big boy said, "and I go to the next lamp post and that's the police phone. I have to telephone for them to send a police car and it comes with its siren going and then I untie you and that's the end of the game."

The big boy went to the next lamp post and pretended to telephone. It took a long time because he told a story about a bank robbery. Then he got a toy police car out of his pocket and started pushing it along the walls of the houses and making a loud siren noise. When he was going past one of the houses a door opened just behind him and a boy came out with a two-wheeler bike. The boy jumped on the bike, rang the bell and rolled off down the sloping street with his legs sticking straight out.

When the big boy heard the bell he turned round.

"Oi!" he shouted, "Oi! Mick!" He pushed the police car in his pocket and ran after the bike. "Oi! Enty! Where're you going?"

"Buy a new pump!" shouted the boy on the bike without looking round. He put his feet on the pedals and pedalled round the corner standing up. The big boy ran after him and vanished round the corner too.

Josie Smith, tied to the lamp post, waited.

He couldn't just forget he'd left her there tied to the lamp post, could he? He'd promised to take her home. He hadn't said Cross my heart and hope to die, but he'd promised. Or perhaps he hadn't promised, perhaps he'd only said. That wasn't the same. Josie Smith waited quietly for a long time but the big boy didn't come.

She thought of counting up to a hundred like he'd said before. Last time she'd only got up to twenty, but this time she went on counting and counting. She even shut her eyes.

"Ninety-seven–ninety-eight–ninety-nine–a hundred."

She opened her eyes. The big boy still didn't come. Something else came. All of a sudden it went dark and when Josie Smith looked up a big raggedy black cloud had come and covered the clean space between the tops of the roofs and chimneys.

Plop! A big raindrop fell on Josie Smith's head. Plop! Plop! Plop!

It was raining again. Her hood wasn't even up after all that running when she was being a robber.

Plop-plop-plop-plop-plop-plop-plop! Faster and faster.

Josie Smith started to roar and cry. She roared and cried so loud that she couldn't see through her tears and she couldn't hear herself think. The faster it rained the harder she roared and her face got so wet you couldn't tell which were raindrops and which were tears.

"Whatever are you doing there?" said a voice.

But Josie Smith didn't hear and she kept on roaring.

"What's to do with you?" asked the voice.

But Josie Smith didn't hear and she kept on roaring. Somebody was untying Josie Smith's hands but she couldn't see through her tears and she couldn't stop roaring.

"Are you going to tell me what's to do?" said the voice.

"I'm lost!" roared Josie Smith, and then she roared louder.

"Lost?" said the voice, and laughed. "Well, well, you must live miles and miles away from here then! Where do you live?"

"Across from Mrs Chadwick's!" roared Josie Smith.

"Is that right?" said the voice. "Across from Mrs Chadwick's. Now shut up, Josie, and open your eyes and see who's got hold of you."

Josie Smith shut up and opened her eyes. "Mrs Chadwick!" she said.

"That's right," said Mrs Chadwick, "it's Mrs Chadwick. And I'd like to know how you're supposed to be lost when that's my back gate over there and that's your house just beyond. You can see your own chimney from here, well, can't you?"

"Yes," said Josie Smith. Josie Smith's house had two dark brown chimney pots with nice pointy tops like crowns.

"You're a little comic, you are," Mrs Chadwick said. "You're top of the class at school and as bright as a button but you'd drown in half a glass of water left to yourself. Come on."

Mrs Chadwick took hold of Josie Smith's hand and took her to the back gate of the shop.

"I want to go home," said Josie Smith.

"You are going home," Mrs Chadwick said, "but you won't get so wet if you come through my house and cross over to your front door."

Josie Smith had never been in Mrs Chadwick's house. It wasn't frightening like Mrs Whittacker's house. It was warm and posh. The kitchen was tidy and everything was the same colour. In the front room there was a nice soft carpet with flowers on it and glass doors and a lot of ornaments. When they came out into the shop they were behind the counter. Josie Smith liked it there. She would have liked to weigh toffees on Mrs Chadwick's scales and put jam slices into a paper bag with the tongs. It was quite dark in the shop and it said OPEN,

on the inside of the door. Mrs Chadwick switched the light on and opened the ice-cream fridge.

"Would a lolly cheer you up?" she said.

"Yes," said Josie Smith.

It wasn't a red lolly. It was a yellow lolly and they're not so good. They taste the same but you can't use them for lipstick. Josie Smith took the yellow lolly and said Thank you. Then Mrs Chadwick lifted up the flap in the counter for her and she went out of the shop, ringing the bell.

"Mum!" she shouted, running in and

banging the front door of her house, "Mum! I've been lost and there was a frightening boy and a house and Mrs Chadwick found me! Mum!"

"Don't bang the door," said Josie's mum. "How many times do I have to tell you? And take those wellingtons off in the house."

"But Mum! I was nearly sick and a boy tied me to a lamp post and it rained and I've been crying hard!"

Josie's mum put down the frying pan she was holding and turned round.

"What have I told you about playing out in the rain? If you get tonsillitis now you won't be able to have your tonsils out. Look at you! You're wet through. Get your coat off and put a towel round your head—and what are you doing eating a lolly just before your tea?"

Josie Smith took off her wet things and put her slippers on and had her hair dried. Then they had their tea.

After tea, when it was warm and comfortable in the kitchen, Josie Smith said,

"Mum? Will you tell me about going into hospital?"

"Again?" said Josie's mum. "I've told you twenty times."

"But will you?" said Josie Smith, "because I like it."

"All right," said Josie's mum, "come on."

Josie Smith got on her mum's knee and snuggled up, and Josie's mum told her all over again about packing her bag and catching the bus in the afternoon and about all the beds in a line and the ice cream they give you because your throat hurts.

"Mum?" Josie Smith said, remembering, "Eileen says she's having a special present for going into hospital and I hate her, she's horrible."

"Why is she horrible?" said Josie's mum. "Because she's having a present?"

"No," said Josie Smith, "because she was horrible today. Everything was horrible today."

"Why is that?" asked Josie's mum. "I thought you liked playing at Eileen's."

"We didn't play at Eileen's", Josie Smith said. "We went to Mrs Whittacker's and Eileen and Dora Whittacker went in a room and played the piano."

"Well, that's nice."

"It wasn't nice, it was horrible," said Josie Smith, "because I was frightened of the house and there was coloured glass and I ran away and then I was lost."

"How could you get lost?" said Josie's mum. "You can see the corner of our house from Mrs Whittacker's front room window."

"We weren't in the front room," Josie Smith said, "and there was a dirt road outside and a brown dog ate my dolly mixtures."

"Did he now?" said Josie's mum. "Well, if that's all that happened, it wasn't so horrible."

"It was," said Josie Smith. "And then a big boy played cops and robbers with me."

"What big boy?" said Josie's mum.

"A big boy who plays with Mick Entwistle and his mum gets frocks from you."

"Oh, that'll be Betty Rawlinson's little boy," said Josie's mum.

"He's not a little boy," Josie Smith said. "He's a big boy and he's got big dirty fists and he said he'd thump me."

"And did he thump you?"

"No," said Josie Smith. "He forgot me and Mrs Chadwick came and took me to her house and gave me a lolly."

"And I suppose the lolly was horrible too," said Josie's mum, and she started laughing.

"Don't laugh at me!" shouted Josie Smith.

"I can't help it," said Josie's mum. "Go on, tell me the lolly was horrible as well. Was it?"

Josie Smith thought and then she said, "It was a yellow lolly and I only like red ones!" And she started laughing as well. She didn't know why but she did. And the more she kept shouting, "It was a horrible day!" the more they both laughed. And by the time they'd finished laughing it was bedtime and the horrible day had gone.

JOSIE SMITH AND THE DANCING CLASS

After school on Monday Josie Smith ran all the way home with Eileen and rushed in through her own front door.

"Mum!" she shouted, banging the door. "Mum! Mum, guess what!"

"Don't bang the door," said Josie's mum. "How many times do I have to tell you? Your face is all red, you've been running."

Josie's mum was sewing buttons on somebody's new frock. "Wash your hands," she said.

Josie Smith washed her hands at the kitchen sink and then she looked at the frock.

"Don't touch," said Josie's mum.

"I'm not," said Josie Smith. "I don't like it. Is it for Eileen's mum?"

"No," said Josie's mum, "it's for a new lady up the street. Did you wash your face?""Yes," said Josie Smith, but she said it with her eyes shut. Her mum kept on sewing and didn't notice. "It's a horrible colour, that frock," she said, "and it looks itchy as well."

"It's a nice tan wool," said Josie's mum, "for the autumn. And there's a bit of stuff left that would make a skirt for you."

"Why is tan for the autumn?" asked Josie Smith.

"Like the leaves," said Josie's mum, "when they start going brown. Set the table for tea."

Josie Smith set the table. "If I were a grown-up lady," she said, "I'd never have brown frocks, I'd have pale blue net ones. And sometimes I'd have sequins and glitter on them and shoes with really high heels like Mrs Chadwick from the shop when she went to a dance." Then she remembered and said, "Mum? You haven't guessed what."

"I can't guess," said Josie's mum, "not while I'm sewing. You'll have to tell me."

"We're having a dancing class at school," Josie Smith said, "and a lady's going to come and teach ballet dancing and Mrs Ormerod's going to play the piano. Can I go?"

"How much is it going to cost?" said Josie's mum.

"I don't know," said Josie Smith. "It depends how many people come and then we'll get a note to bring home. Can I go?"

"We'll see," said Josie's mum.

"Why do you always say We'll see?" said Josie Smith.

"Because we'll have to see," said Josie's mum. "Now eat your tea."

When she went to bed, Josie Smith snuggled up to her big woolly panda and said, "Percy, there's a dancing class and I'm going, and when I grow up I'm going to be a ballet dancer." She closed her eyes and wished as hard as she could that her mum would let her. Then she fell asleep. The next day, when they were walking to school, Eileen said, "I'm going to the dancing class and my mum says I can wear my ballet frock if I want and I'm having some new ballet shoes."

Eileen already had some ballet shoes, Josie Smith knew she had. She got them to go with her Little Bo-Peep costume when they went to a fancy dress party at Christmas. Josie Smith didn't say anything. Then Eileen said, "I'm having pink ones with ribbons."

Josie Smith shut her eyes a bit and said, "So am I."

When they were lining up in the yard, Gary Grimes pushed in near Josie Smith and Eileen and said, "I'm going to the new dancing class."

"You are not!" Eileen said. "Boys don't go to dancing classes, stupid."

"Oh yes they do, stupid," Gary Grimes said. "Miss Potts said anybody could go and she's the headmistress. And if Josie Smith's going, I'm going."

"So? Who says Josie Smith's going?" Eileen said.

"I bet anything she is," Gary Grimes said, "because she's always drawing ballet dancers. I've seen her. Are you going?" he said to Josie Smith.

"Yes I am," said Josie Smith, keeping her eyes a bit shut.

"And she's having new pink ballet shoes," Eileen said, "the same as me."

Then their line started going in. In the classroom they made a terrible noise because everybody was shouting and laughing and jumping about.

"Quiet!" Miss Valentine said. "Quiet, everybody!" And when they didn't stop laughing she said, "What are you all laughing about?"

"It's Gary Grimes," Rawley Baxter said. "He wants to go to a dancing class with a load of girls!"

"Well, why shouldn't he?" Miss Valentine said. She made them sit in their places and then she said, "Some of the most famous ballet dancers in the world are men.

You have to have more muscles to be a ballet dancer than you do to be a footballer, did you know that?"

"No, Miss Valentine," everybody said. All except Rawley Baxter who whispered to himself, "That's stupid!" And he flew his plastic Batman over their table.

"I'll see if I can find some pictures to put up for you," Miss Valentine said. "Now, let's get started with our sums."

Josie Smith hated sums. She always got them wrong. But today she didn't care anyway because all morning she thought about the dancing class and about new pink ballet shoes, just as if her mum had said Yes instead of We'll see. After playtime they had reading and after dinner they had drawing and Josie Smith drew a ballet dancer with her arms high above her head and a tiny crown in her hair.

"Will you draw me one?" Eileen said.

"You'd better draw Gary Grimes one as well," Rawley Baxter said, and he laughed until his face went all red because he couldn't stop.

"Just you give over!" said Gary Grimes.

"Grimesy on his tippy toes!" Rawley Baxter said and he kept on laughing.

Eileen started laughing at Gary Grimes as well, and he put his fist up and said, "You just wait! You've got to go into hospital and they'll stick needles in you and cut you up with knives."

"Quiet at that table," Miss Valentine said.

Rawley Baxter stopped laughing and drew a picture of Batman zooming up on to the roof of a skyscraper. Miss Valentine let them take their drawings home.

When they were lined up near the classroom door with their coats on and their drawings in their hands Miss Valentine said, "That's lovely, Josie. I bet you'll be going to the dancing class, won't you?"

"Yes," said Josie Smith, and she didn't even shut her eyes, so it would have to be true. Then they went home.

Sometimes, when you want something really hard you have to pester for it. Other times it's better if you're just good. Josie

Smith tried to be good. After tea she went to the library with her mum and she chose a big book with pictures of ballet dancers in it but she didn't say anything. She just sat quietly in the library that was warm and smelt of shiny new shelves and polish. Going home in the cold she did hold the big book so that her mum would see what it was but she didn't say anything. Her mum only said, "The nights are drawing in."

"What does that mean?" Josie Smith said.

"It means it's getting dark earlier," said

Josie's mum. "It's autumn. Can't you smell it in the air?"

Josie Smith put her face up and sniffed. "I can smell the fish and chip shop," she said.

"You would," said Josie's mum. "You're a little comic."

When they got home and Josie's mum said it was bedtime, Josie Smith didn't say Aw, mum! She went straight upstairs to get ready for bed and Ginger the cat followed her.

"I don't know what to do, Ginger," Josie Smith said. "I'm being as good as I can so my mum'll say I can go to dancing class. But if I ask her if I can go I'll be pestering so I won't be being good any more."

Ginger blinked.

Josie Smith got in bed with her big book. Then she got out again to pick her kilt and cardigan off the floor and fold them up. There are so many things to remember when you're being good and Josie Smith wasn't so good at remembering things.

When you remember to clean your teeth you get shouted at for squeezing the toothpaste in the wrong place. When you try to eat the horrible lumpy bits in your dinner and pretend to like them you get shouted at for putting too much in your mouth. Josie Smith got back in bed and lay with her eyes open, thinking. Ginger curled himself up in his basket and lay with his eyes open without blinking. Then they both fell asleep.

When Josie Smith and Eileen walked into their classroom next day they were giggling and whispering like they always did. Then they stopped.

"Ooh!" whispered Josie Smith, and she stared.

"Ooh!" whispered Eileen, and she stared.

Then everybody stopped and stared. Miss Valentine had put two big posters on the wall. One showed a ballerina in a white frock and shoes and white roses in her hair. The other one showed a man in a black cloak with a sword and he was flying through the air like a rocket.

"Eh! Look at that!" Rawley Baxter said.

"Yes, look at it," Miss Valentine said, "That's what ballet dancers can do, Rawley. I bet you wish you could jump like that."

Rawley Baxter didn't say anything. All day he kept looking at the flying dancer. When Miss Valentine gave them some paper to write a story with a picture he didn't write anything. Rawley Baxter never wrote anything. He only drew pictures of Batman. Today he drew Batman flying through the air with a sword like the man in the poster. Josie Smith drew a picture of Sleeping Beauty with a crown on in bed with a panda next to her and a cat in a basket near the bed. Eileen copied off Josie Smith.

Then Miss Potts came in.

"Excuse me, Miss Valentine," she shouted, marching across the room with some papers in her hand. "Now, all of you listen to me!"

Josie Smith felt her face go hot and her chest go bam bam bam! She knew what

Miss Potts had come for. She'd come to count the people going to the dancing class and give out the notes to take home.

"Come to me," roared Miss Potts, "all the children who want to join the dancing class. There's a note for your mothers to sign!"

Eileen got up and went. Ann Lomax and Julie Horrocks got up and went. Even Gary Grimes got up and went. Josie Smith got up and stood still near her table. She didn't know what to do. Her mum hadn't said Yes. But if she didn't take the note home it would be too late. Then Rawley Baxter got up and went.

"You?" shouted Miss Potts.

Rawley Baxter didn't say anything.

"Well, see that you behave yourself! I don't want to hear about you causing trouble. Is that understood?"

Rawley Baxter didn't say anything.

"Is that understood?" roared Miss Potts.

"I won't cause any trouble," Rawley Baxter said. He looked at the poster of the flying ballet dancer and then he went and sat down holding his note and his plastic Batman. Josie Smith stood still where she was. She felt hot and frightened. She wanted to go to the dancing class so much that it made a big pain in her head and her chest and her hands felt sticky.

Miss Potts put a few more notes down on Miss Valentine's desk in case there was anybody away and then she marched out, shouting, "Thank you, Miss Valentine!"

At hometime they stood in a line by the classroom door and Miss Valentine said, "Now, don't forget your note if you've got one. Rawley Baxter, where's yours?"

"It's in my pocket," he said.

Gary Grimes was holding his; it was all dirty and sticky.

"I've got my note," Eileen said.

"I've got my note," Ann Lomax said.

"And I've got mine," Julie Horrocks said.

Then Miss Valentine said, "Josie Smith, where's your note?"

Josie Smith looked at Miss Valentine but she didn't say anything. She felt sick.

"What's the matter with you?" Miss Valentine said.

And in a very small voice Josie Smith said, "I feel sick."

"I know what the matter is," Miss Valentine said. "You've lost your note, haven't you?"Josie Smith didn't say anything.

"I saw you get up when Miss Potts came in," Miss Valentine said, "and I know you wouldn't miss the dancing class, now would you?"

In an even tinier voice Josie Smith said, "No."

"Well? Where is it then?" Miss Valentine said.

Josie Smith didn't say anything. She was nearly crying. Then Miss Valentine patted her on the head and said, "Don't get so upset about things. It's not the end of the world if you've lost it." And she went to her desk and got one of the spare notes and gave it to Josie Smith.

"Good afternoon, everybody," Miss Valentine said.

"Goo-daf-ter-noon-Miss Valen-tine," everybody said. And then they all went home.

After tea, Josie's mum said, "I'm just slipping round to the lady at number twenty to measure this hem. Do you want to come?"

"No," said Josie Smith, because she didn't like the tan wool frock very much. "I want to read my book."

"I'll not be five minutes," said Josie's mum, and she put on her coat and went.

Josie Smith waited a bit and then she went and got the note from her coat pocket

and put it carefully on the mantelpiece. That was where she always put notes from school so that her mum would see them and not forget them. Even if she didn't ask about dancing class her mum would see the note there and that wouldn't be pestering.

But when Josie's mum came back she only said, "Get to bed." She didn't see the note. She didn't even look at the mantelpiece. Upstairs in bed, Josie Smith held Percy tight to her chest and listened but she couldn't hear her mum opening the note.

"What shall I do, Percy?" she whispered, and then she said, "You stay here in the warm." And she got out of bed and sat at the top of the stairs. She sat there for a very long time until her feet were freezing and her knees were stiff and her eyes were tired and scratchy but she didn't hear her mum open the note.

Josie Smith got back in bed and held Percy's big woolly head close to hers. "I don't know what to do, Percy," she whispered in his soft ear, "if my mum hasn't seen the note in the morning." She sniffed Percy's clean fur and hugged him for a long time until at last she fell asleep.

The next morning, Josie Smith was so tired that she went downstairs with her buttons done up all wrong and she forgot to look on the mantelpiece. She was half asleep.

"Fasten your cardigan properly," said Josie's mum. "Eat your breakfast. What are you daydreaming about? You're going to be late. Get your coat – and where's your other glove? Put a scarf on. And think on, you go straight to school and no messing, it's late. And see that you give this note in and don't lose it on the way."

Josie Smith woke up.

"Am I going to the dancing class?" she said.

"You said you wanted to," said Josie's mum.

"I do want to!" shouted Josie Smith, and she ran out, banging the door.

Walking up to school Eileen said, "I've brought my note and my new ballet shoes, have you?"

"Yes," said Josie Smith, shutting her eyes a bit because she'd only brought the note.

After they went into the classroom, Miss Potts came round and collected their notes. She told Rawley Baxter there wouldn't be a second chance for him if he made any trouble.

Out in the yard at dinner time Ann Lomax came up to Josie Smith and Eileen and said, "I've brought my note and my new ballet shoes, have you?"

"I have," Eileen said.

Josie Smith didn't say anything.

When it was hometime, Miss Valentine said, "Those of you who are staying behind for dancing, change your shoes and go into the hall. Everybody else get their coats on. Good afternoon, children."

"Goo-daf-ter-noon-Miss-Val-en-tine!" everybody said.

When the other children had gone home Eileen got a little bag from her coathook and took out her new ballet shoes and her ballet frock.

"You don't have to have a ballet frock," Ann Lomax said, because she hadn't got one.

Josie Smith stood in the corner near the door and she didn't say anything.

Julie Horrocks came up to her and said, "I'm wearing my gym shoes because Miss Potts said. Are you?"

Josie Smith nodded but she didn't say anything. She didn't want to wear her

horrible black gym shoes, she wanted pink
ballet shoes like Eileen and Ann Lomax.
Julie Horrocks got her gym shoes out from
her pigeon hole under the bench and put
them on. Julie Horrocks always wore a
check skirt that was too long so that nobody
would notice her long thin legs.

"Why are you not putting your gym
shoes on?" Julie Horrocks said.

Josie Smith didn't say anything.

Gary Grimes and Rawley Baxter were
fighting.

"Just get off, Grimesy!" yelled Rawley
Baxter. "They're mine! Push off and find
your own!" And he grabbed the gym shoes
from Gary Grimes's hand.

"Quiet, now!" Miss Valentine said, and
then she went out.

Eileen was dressed in her white ballet
frock and her pink ballet shoes but she
couldn't tie the ribbons on the shoes so she
went into the hall with them trailing on the
floor behind her. Ann Lomax tied her
ribbons in a big floppy bow at the front and
they came undone as she walked into the

hall and trailed on the floor behind her. Rawley Baxter was wearing his gym

shoes and his Batman cloak and mask and carrying a big sword made of cardboard and silver paper and he marched into the hall making Batman noises to himself.

Gary Grimes ran after him, limping and shouting, "Ouch! Ouch! My feet!"

Rawley Baxter turned round to tell him to shut up, and then the door slammed behind them.

Josie Smith stood in the classroom behind the door by herself and wished and wished and wished that she had some pink ballet shoes and she hated Ann Lomax and Eileen. Then she heard someone clapping their hands in the hall and a lady's voice said, "Come and stand here, all of you, in a straight line in front of me."

It must be the new dancing teacher! It was late. Josie Smith ran over to her pigeon hole to get her horrible black gym shoes out. She poked her hand in and didn't find them. She crouched down and looked but there was nothing there. Josie Smith's chest went bam bam bam! She heard the teacher clap her hands again and she opened the door just a bit to peep. The dancing teacher was standing in front of the stage. She had her hair in a bun and she was smiling. The children stood in a long line in front of her. There were a lot of girls from all the other classes and Josie Smith didn't know what they were called. Gary Grimes and Rawley Baxter were the only boys in the line and everybody had their gym shoes on except Ann Lomax and Eileen and nobody except Eileen had a ballet frock.

If only Josie Smith had found her gym shoes! But there she was in her wellingtons, hiding behind the door.

The teacher told the children that she was called Miss Pendlebury. Then she pointed to Eileen and said, "What's your name?"

"Eileen," said Eileen.

"Well, Eileen," Miss Pendlebury said, "that's a very pretty ballet dress but you mustn't wear it to come to lessons. Sometimes we'll be doing exercises on the floor and it would get spoiled, now wouldn't it? You keep it at home and save it for

special occasions. And if you want to wear ballet shoes take off those ribbons and ask your mums to sew some elastic across the front. If you've only got gym shoes that's all right."

Josie Smith stayed where she was in her wellingtons, peeping.

Then Miss Pendlebury noticed Rawley Baxter.

"What's your name?" Miss Pendlebury said. "Rawley Baxter," Rawley Baxter said.

"Well, Rawley Baxter," Miss

Pendlebury said, "You look very smart but why are you wearing a cloak and a mask and carrying a sword?"

"For the jumping," Rawley Baxter said.

"Oh," Miss Pendlebury said. "Well, perhaps you'd like to put your cloak and sword on the chair over there for a minute. We won't be doing any jumping for a long time. Today we're going to learn the first three positions of the feet."

Rawley Baxter didn't move.

"Rawley?" Miss Pendlebury said.

"It's all right," Rawley Baxter said, "I'll wait." He went to the side of the room and stood with his feet apart, holding his sword tight, waiting.

Josie Smith stood where she was in her wellingtons, peeping.

Miss Pendlebury didn't know what to do about Rawley Baxter. Nobody ever knew what to do about Rawley Baxter. He went on standing at the side and Miss Pendlebury carried on.

"First position," Miss Pendlebury said, "turn out your toes like this." The long line of children turned out their toes and Gary Grimes said, "Ow!"

"Don't overdo it," Miss Pendlebury said, "it'll hurt a bit at first."

Behind the classroom door, not overdoing it, Josie Smith in her wellingtons turned out her toes like the others. Rawley Baxter just watched.

"Second position," Miss Pendlebury said, "with your feet apart, like this."

The long line of children pointed a toe and stood with their feet apart.

"That's the way," Miss Pendlebury said. And Gary Grimes said, "Ow!"

Behind the classroom door Josie Smith pointed a wellington and stood with her feet apart. Rawley Baxter just watched.

"Third position," Miss Pendlebury said, "with your right foot in front like this."

The long line of children put their right foot in front and Gary Grimes screamed, Ow! Ow! Ow!

"Whatever's the matter?" Miss Pendlebury said. "It can't hurt as much as that."

"It can if your shoes are too small," Rawley Baxter shouted from the side. "They're not his!"

"Ow!" shouted Gary Grimes. He started crying.

"Take no notice of him, Miss," shouted Rawley Baxter from the side, "he's soft."

"Be quiet!" Miss Pendlebury told him. "And you —what's your name? Come here."

Gary Grimes limped over to Miss Pendlebury and took off the shoes that were hurting him.

"Whose are these gym shoes?" Miss Pendlebury asked him.

"I don't know!" roared Gary Grimes. He was still crying.

Miss Pendlebury looked inside the shoes. "J. Smith," she read. "Who's that?"

Behind the classroom door, Josie Smith in her wellingtons kept quiet.

Nobody told Miss Pendlebury who J. Smith was, but Josie Smith saw Eileen look round and then whisper something in Ann Lomax's ear.

After that Gary Grimes did the

exercises in his stockinged feet. Josie Smith did them behind the door in her wellingtons and Rawley Baxter watched.

At home after tea, Josie's mum said, "Did you like your dancing class?"

"Not very much," said Josie Smith, "because Gary Grimes pinched my gym shoes."

"Well, see that you get them back," said Josie's mum, "I can't afford to buy you another pair."

"I have got them back," Josie Smith said. "He left them on the floor."

"Well, what are you looking so miserable about, then?" said Josie's mum. "Did something else happen?"

"No," said Josie Smith with her eyes half shut.

"You didn't lose your note, did you?"

"No," said Josie Smith.

"You didn't forget to give it in, then?"

"No," said Josie Smith.

"Have you been fighting with Eileen?"

"No," said Josie Smith, but her face was white and she had a lump in her throat.

"Well, in that case," Josie's mum said, looking at her hard, "I just hope you're not getting tonsillitis right when it's time for you to go into hospital."

"I don't want to have my tonsils out with Eileen," Josie Smith said. "I hate Eileen!"

"I thought as much," said Josie's mum. "You have been fighting with Eileen. Come on. Get your coat on and come with me. I've got a surprise for you that might cheer you up."

"Where are we going?" asked Josie Smith.

"We're just slipping round to number twenty," said Josie's mum, "to take this tan frock. It's finished."

"That's not a surprise," said Josie Smith, "I've seen it before." But she didn't want to stay at home by herself so she put her coat on. It was nearly dark outside. They went up the street together and Josie's mum carried the tan wool frock in a polythene bag over her arm.

When the door of number twenty

opened, a lady's voice said, "Oh, how nice. Come on in."

When they were in the front room the lady's voice said, "And who's this?"

Then Josie Smith looked up at her.

It was a tall nice lady with her hair in a bun. It was Miss Pendlebury!

Josie Smith's chest went bam bam bam because she was frightened. Would Miss Pendlebury know she'd done the lesson standing behind the door in her wellingtons?

What if somebody had told her? What if Eileen had told?

"Has the cat got your tongue?" said Josie's mum.

"No," said Josie Smith in a tiny voice.

"I thought you'd be surprised," said Josie's mum.

Miss Pendlebury looked very hard at Josie Smith. Josie Smith got hold of her mum's coat with one fist.

"I don't remember seeing you today," Miss Pendlebury said. "Didn't your mum tell me you were coming to my class?"

"Yes," whispered Josie Smith.

Miss Pendlebury looked at Josie's mum and shook her head. "She didn't come, Mrs Smith," Miss Pendlebury said.

"I did! I did come!" and just to show them she pointed her toes in her wellingtons and said, "I learnt the first position."

Miss Pendlebury stared at her and said, "And the second? And the third?"

Josie Smith in her wellingtons did them all.

"But where were you standing?" Miss

Pendlebury said, "if I didn't see you?"

Josie Smith got closer to her mum and said, "Behind my classroom door because Gary Grimes... Because Gary Grimes..." But Josie Smith never told over people so she stopped telling and started to cry.

Miss Pendlebury bent down and took hold of Josie Smith's shoulders.

"What's your first name?" she asked her.

"Josie," said Josie Smith.

"J. Smith," said Miss Pendlebury, "I

see. So that boy whose feet hurt was wearing your gym shoes, wasn't he?"

"Yes," said Josie Smith.

"But why didn't you come and tell me?" Miss Pendlebury said, "instead of hiding?"

"I don't know," said Josie Smith.

"Come with me," Miss Pendlebury said. She took Josie Smith's hand and they went upstairs to the back bedroom where there was a great big wardrobe. Miss Pendlebury opened it, and inside it was full of ballet

frocks, rows and rows of them, white and turquoise and pink and blue. And there were shelves at the side full of shoes and ribbons and hairnets and wreathes of flowers and a jumble of coloured tights.

"My little girl's grown up," Miss Pendlebury said. "She's a real dancer now on the stage and I never could throw her old things away. I'm sure there'll be a pair of shoes to fit you."

And there was.

They weren't pink like Eileen's, they were red and they had elastic, not ribbons. Miss Pendlebury said red or black shoes were best for practising because they had to work very hard and would soon get dirty. Then she gave Josie Smith a little velvety red net to hold her hair in a bun and showed her how to wear it.

When they were going back down the street in the dark, Josie's mum said, "Didn't I say you'd get a surprise?"

Josie Smith didn't say anything. She was holding the ballet shoes so tight to her chest that she could hardly breathe.

Every night she slept with the red ballet shoes and the net under her pillow and every night she showed them to Percy before they went to sleep.

When it was the day for dancing class, Josie's mum said, "Take that kilt off, you can wear your new skirt today."

It was a full skirt, the colour of autumn leaves. Josie Smith didn't say it was a horrible colour. She didn't say it was scratchy. She only said, "Will Miss Pendlebury be wearing hers?"

"How should I know that?" said Josie's mum. "Fasten your cardigan."

Miss Pendlebury wasn't wearing hers, but when she asked them who could remember the first three positions nobody could. Nobody except Josie Smith, who put her hand up.

"What've you put your hand up for, stupid?" whispered Eileen. "You can't remember. You never came!"

But Josie Smith, in her red shoes and a bun with red velvet net, went out to the front and showed them.

"Well, that's funny," Miss Pendlebury said. "I don't remember seeing you at the first lesson. Do any of you remember seeing her?"

She looked along the long line of girls and at Gary Grimes in his stockinged feet and at Rawley Baxter with his cloak and sword standing at the side, waiting. Nobody remembered seeing Josie Smith.

"In that case," Miss Pendlebury said, "you must have magic shoes that know what to do. Perhaps they've done a lot of dancing before." And while they were all laughing she looked at Josie Smith and winked.

JOSIE SMITH
IN HOSPITAL

The night before Josie Smith had to go into hospital she had a bath.

"Swim me up and down," she said to her mum, "and tell me about having my tonsils out."

"I've told you a hundred times," said Josie's mum. "Now, wash your ears."

"I have washed my ears," said Josie Smith. "Tell me again."

Josie's mum squeezed out the face cloth and washed Josie Smith's ears properly and swam her up and down and told her again about going into hospital.

"You're going to set off at two o'clock."

"And Eileen," said Josie Smith.

"And Eileen," said Josie's mum.

"And Percy," said Josie Smith.

"And Percy," said Josie's mum.

"And your bag's all packed," said Josie's mum, "with pyjamas and dressing gown and your slippers with pompoms on and your toothbrush and soap and sponge and towel."

"And my story book and my ballet shoes," said Josie Smith.

"And your story book and your ballet shoes," said Josie's mum.

"And I'm carrying my bag myself," said Josie Smith. "I bet Eileen's not." Then she said, "Mum? Eileen says she's having a present specially for going into hospital."

"Eileen's always having presents," said Josie's mum.

"But is she having a special present?" asked Josie Smith. "A secret one like she said?"

"How should I know?" said Josie's mum. "You know what she's like. She's probably having a doll dressed as a nurse to take."

Josie Smith didn't care so much if it

was only a doll dressed as a nurse. She didn't like fancy dolls, she liked baby dolls and anyway, she was taking Percy and he was better than any doll.

"Tell me about the ice cream," she said.

"You won't be living on nothing but ice cream, you know," said Josie's mum. "But they'll probably give you some the day after you've had your operation because it's nice and smooth for your throat. Now, stand up and let me dry you."

Josie Smith stood up to be wrapped in the big towel.

"I can dry myself," she said.

"You forget your ears and toes," said Josie's mum.

"I know, but you rub too hard," said Josie Smith. "Do I have to have my tonsils out with Eileen?"

"We asked specially for you to go in together," said Josie's mum. "You don't want to go in hospital by yourself, do you?"

"I don't know," said Josie Smith. "I want to go in with Eileen because she's my best friend, but sometimes she's horrible and I don't like her so much because she's having a special present and I'm not."

"Never you mind about Eileen's present," said Josie's mum. "It'll be something silly, you wait and see. Get your pyjamas on."

Josie Smith got her pyjamas on and went to bed. Percy was there with his back to her.

"Percy," said Josie Smith, rolling him over so his big furry ear was close to her face, "I want to tell you something." She snuggled close to his big woolly head and whispered to him about Eileen's present.

"But I don't care," she said, hugging him tight, "because you're coming with me." And she sniffed his clean fur and fell asleep.

When Josie Smith woke up she felt excited but she couldn't remember why. It wasn't Christmas, it wasn't her birthday, what was it?

"I'm having my tonsils out!" she remembered, and she was excited all morning because she was going into hospital. It was a specially long morning. It always is when you're waiting for the afternoon. Josie Smith read a whole book and did some cutting out and unpacked all the things in her case and packed them up again, and it was still morning. Then she practised all the ballet steps she knew and it was still morning but she could smell her dinner. Then she went upstairs and read Percy a story and brushed his fur and her mum shouted, "Josie! Come and get your dinner!"

After dinner Josie Smith got dressed in

a clean blouse and her kilt and a clean fawn cardigan and clean fawn socks.

"Put your shoes on," said Josie's mum.

Josie Smith looked at the shoes. They were brown shoes with laces. They were very shiny and the laces were open and the tongues sticking out ready to be put on. When her mum wasn't looking Josie Smith pulled her tongue out back at them. She hated her shoes. They were hard and ugly and as soon as she put them on her mum always said, "Just you be careful how you walk and don't kick the toes in."

Josie Smith looked at her wellingtons standing on the mat by the kitchen door. You don't have to mind how you walk in wellingtons. You can jump in puddles in them and climb trees, and you can't kick the toes in even if you try.

Josie's mum put the shoes on Josie Smith. She only ever wore them on very special days so she never got used to tying the laces.

"Ouch," she said, "ouch!" as the shoes were laced up tight, "I wish I could go in my wellingtons. Why can't I?"

"It's not raining," said Josie's mum. "Your wellingtons will be there waiting for you when you come home."

Josie Smith looked at her wellingtons, and she didn't want to go into hospital any more.

"Eileen's got shoes with ankle straps," she said.

"Eileen's mother has money to throw away," said Josie's mum. "These are sensible shoes that'll last you. Now, mind how you walk or you'll have the toes kicked in."

They put their coats on and went to call for Eileen. Josie Smith carried her own bag and Percy was under her arm.

"We're just getting our coats on," said Eileen's mum, so they went inside and waited. Eileen was in the kitchen.

"Look at me!" she said, and they looked.

Eileen was dressed as a nurse. She was wearing a dark blue frock and a white apron with a red cross on the bib. On top of her yellow curly hair was a white cap and that had a red cross too. On her feet she had brand new white socks with a pink frill round the tops and black patent leather shoes with ankle straps.

"I'm a nurse," Eileen said.

Josie Smith didn't say anything. A big lump came in her throat just like tonsillitis, and she squeezed Percy so hard she was squashing him.

"I'm taking my doll," Eileen said, "and my nurse's case with bandages and things in it."

There on the chair was a pale blue plastic case with a red cross on the front of it. "And," Eileen said, "I've got a special cup and a special comb with my name on them."

Josie Smith didn't say anything. They set off. Eileen only carried her little nurse's case and her mum carried everything else. On the bus Josie Smith felt sick but her mum said it was only because she was excited. She didn't feel excited. She didn't want to go into hospital any more because she hadn't got a nurse's uniform or a case or a cup and a comb with her name on them.

When they got off the bus and went in at the big gates of the hospital, Eileen said to Josie Smith, "As soon as we get there we can play hospitals in a real hospital and I'll be the nurse."

"We can't," Josie Smith said, "because they make you put your pyjamas on, my mum said, and your dressing gown."

"Well," Eileen said, "I'm keeping my uniform on."

They climbed some stairs and went along a high corridor.

"There's a funny smell," Josie Smith said and sniffed.

It was a horrible smell, like school dinner all mixed up with floor polish and the dentist's.

"I don't like it," Eileen said, and she started crying.

"Don't you start crying," said Eileen's mum. "We're here. Look, there's the nurse."

But Eileen was roaring now, and her

mum had to drag her into the big ward. A lot of children were sitting on their beds or sleeping or playing at a table in the middle. They all stopped what they were doing and stared at Eileen. They'd never heard anybody roar so loud.

"Mer-her-her!" roared Eileen, "mer-her-her-her!"

"For goodness' sake!" said Eileen's mum. "She'll settle in a minute," said the nurse.

But Eileen didn't settle. Eileen didn't want to settle. Eileen wanted to go home.

"I don't want to have my tonsils out!" she roared, "I don't want to!"

The nurse looked at Eileen's uniform and bent down to her and said, "What a nice uniform you've got on. You can be a little nurse and help me push my trolley round. You'd like that, wouldn't you?"

"No!" roared Eileen, and instead of pushing the trolley she pushed the nurse as hard as she could and tried to kick her.

"Can't you do anything with her?" the nurse asked Eileen's mum. "She'll upset the other children."

"Nobody can do anything with her," said Eileen's mum, "except Josie Smith. Where is Josie?"

But Josie Smith had gone. They looked all round the ward and saw big children and tiny children and fat children and fast asleep children, all in their pyjamas. But they couldn't see a kilt or a fawn cardigan or the sensible brown shoes anywhere.

"She's run away!" shouted Josie's mum. "Oh! For goodness' sake! She must have run away while we were all looking at

Eileen!" Josie's mum started to run out of the door to look for her.

"Mum!" shouted Josie Smith, "I haven't run away! I'm here!"

Josie's mum came back. "Are you hiding somewhere?" she said.

All the children playing at the table left their toys and laughed. Then they came to Josie's mum and pulled her along and said, "There she is!"

And there she was. In bed in her striped pyjamas with the buttons done up all wrong. "I saw my bed," she said, "with my name on a board at the bottom so I got in and here I am."

And there she was. Reading her book.

And in the next bed, with the covers pulled up to his chin, was Percy.

Eileen saw them and stopped crying.

"Well," said the nurse, "if that panda's here to have his tonsils out, Eileen, I'm afraid you've lost your bed. You'll have to go home and come in another time without your friend Josie."

"I'm not!" shouted Eileen. "It's my

bed!" And she ran towards the bed to throw Percy out. Josie Smith jumped out of bed and rescued him just in time.

"He was only joking," she said to Eileen, "and you haven't to be rough with Percy because if he gets ripped his stuffing'll come out."

But Eileen wasn't listening. She was getting undressed as fast as she could and her mum was unpacking all her fancy things. Josie's mum unbuttoned Josie Smith's pyjamas and buttoned them up again properly. Then she started packing Josie

Smith's clothes to take them home.

"I've put my ballet shoes in the locker," Josie Smith said, "and my slippers."

When the nurse came she said, "I can see you're going to be a good girl. When I've got everybody settled you can get up and play." Then she saw all the things Eileen's mum was unpacking and she whispered to Josie's mum, "She's brought enough stuff for ten children."

"She's got a pink cup with her name on it," Josie Smith said, "and a comb with her name on it as well."

"She would have," whispered the nurse, and she winked. "You have a little natter with your mum now and I'll see you later."

Josie Smith sat straight up in bed looking at all the other children in all the other beds. "Will they bring us our ice cream now?" she said.

"No," said Josie's mum, "that's for after you've had your tonsils out. But remember, I didn't promise. They might give you something else that's soft and doesn't hurt your throat, like jelly."

"But not blancmange," said Josie Smith, "I hate blancmange because it always has little lumps in it, and Percy doesn't like it either. I'm glad I'm having my tonsils out."

Josie's mum stroked her head and said, "Don't get too excited or you won't get to sleep tonight."

They had chicken soup and salad and a square piece of cake for tea. Then they had a little wash and Josie Smith got back into bed in her striped pyjamas and Eileen got into bed in her pink and white nightie with rosebuds on it. Josie's mum and Eileen's mum put on their coats to go.

"Next time we see you," said Josie's mum, "you'll have no tonsils!"

"And I won't have to wear my itchy scarf to stop me getting tonsillitis!" shouted Josie Smith. She waved to her mum and Eileen cried and then the nurse came round.

"Come on," she said, "put your dressing gowns on and come and watch telly for half an hour until the doctor comes round."

Eileen stopped crying, and they sat on little chairs with some other children, watching cartoons until the doctor came.

"Aaagh!" said Josie Smith, opening her mouth wide for the doctor with a fat pink face. "Aaagh!" And he pressed on her tongue with a lolly stick just like Dr Gleason at home. Then he put tubes in his ears and listened to her chest and back and then he looked at Percy and said, "Who's this chap? He's bigger than you."

"It's Percy," said Josie Smith.

"And is Percy in for tonsils, too?"

"That's right," said the nurse, coming to help Josie Smith with her buttons, "and he wanted a bed to himself, as well."

"I'd better just listen to his heart, then," the doctor said, and he put the tubes back in his ears and listened to Percy's chest and back.

"He seems to be all right," the doctor said. "You bring him down with you in the morning and we'll whip his tonsils out with yours and then you'll both feel better." Then he laughed and patted Josie Smith's head and said, "Who's next?"

Eileen started crying.

Eileen cried until bedtime. There was a little boy who cried a lot, as well, right down at the other end of the ward. The nurse told Josie Smith that he was only four and very poorly so he couldn't help it. She said Eileen ought to be brave like Josie Smith. Then she said Goodnight and see you tomorrow because the night nurse was coming.

Josie Smith was glad she was brave. She was glad she was having her tonsils out. She was glad she was in hospital.

Then the lights went out.

It wasn't all dark because you could just see the other white beds and the lamp that was lit on the nurse's desk. But it was too dark to read and Josie Smith always read before she went to sleep. She had her book in bed with her but she couldn't even see the pictures. She closed the book and held its shiny cover tight to her chest and snuggled closer to Percy. Then she poked her head up and whispered, "Eileen!" But Eileen had gone to sleep. The poorly little boy must have gone to sleep, too, because he'd stopped crying. It was very quiet.

There were some noises, though. Echo noises a long way away that Josie Smith couldn't understand. She put her head under the bedclothes so she wouldn't hear them. The bed had a funny rubbery smell like new wellingtons, not like a real bed. And you couldn't snuggle down because the sheets were hard and tight.

"Percy," whispered Josie Smith into Percy's furry ear, "I don't like it so much now. I don't think I want to have my tonsils out any more but we can't go home by ourselves in the dark. You have to go on a bus."

Josie Smith lay in her bed, holding Percy tight and thinking.

She tried hard to think of nice things. She wanted to think about Miss Pendlebury and the red ballet shoes in her locker but instead she thought, What if you wake up when they're taking your tonsils out? Her mum had said she'd be fast asleep, but she should have been fast asleep now and she wasn't. Everybody else was, but she wasn't. She tried to think about her mum and about her wellingtons waiting on the mat to go out playing, and a perfect piece of silver paper she'd saved up for cutting out. But instead she kept thinking that tomorrow she was going to have to swallow a pill, her mum had said. She wondered if she'd be able to swallow it. She wasn't very good at swallowing pills.

It was very hot. Josie Smith wished she could get to sleep. Then she must have gone to sleep because she saw the big doctor with the pink face. She was standing looking at him in a long long room dressed in her kilt and wellingtons and holding Percy, so she knew it must be a dream because her kilt and wellingtons were at home and she was in bed in her pyjamas. It must be a dream but it looked real. The doctor held out his hand and she had to give him Percy. The doctor said, "We'll just whip his tonsils out." And he started undoing Percy's stitching so he fell to pieces and all his stuffing came out. Josie Smith started crying in her dream. Then she woke up. She was still crying. They were real tears, not dream tears, but she wasn't making a noise. She dried her cheeks on Percy and held him tight.

"It's all right," she whispered to him, "it was only a dream. You don't have to be frightened. I wish it wasn't so hot and dark. I wish we could go home." But she still didn't make a noise. She lay with her eyes wide open, trying not to go back to sleep so she wouldn't have another frightening dream. But even with her eyes open the dream didn't go away properly. You have to put the light on and your mum has to come to make a horrible dream go away. So she kept thinking of the doctor getting hold of Percy and seeing Percy with his stuffing coming out. She held his big soft head and more and more tears came and wet her cheeks and Percy's cheeks and the stiff pillow.

"Poor Percy," she whispered. "It's all my fault for bringing you. I should have left you at home with my mum. I should have come by myself. You don't have to have your tonsils out. I won't let anybody touch you."

"Whatever's the matter with you?" asked a quiet voice, and a light shone in Josie Smith's eyes. She blinked. The light went out and somebody sat down on Josie Smith's bed. It was the night nurse. She was holding a torch in the lap of her apron.

"You're crying," she said.

"I tried not to make a noise," Josie Smith said, sniffing.

"You didn't make a noise," said the nurse, "I was just going round checking that you were all asleep. Do you want to tell me

what you're crying for?" She put her cool hand on Josie Smith's forehead. "You're red hot!" she said. "You are upsetting yourself. Here." She took a tissue from her pocket and said, "Blow."

Josie Smith blew.

"Now then," said the nurse, "tell me all about it."

"I don't want Percy to have his tonsils out with me," Josie Smith said.

"And who's Percy? I didn't see anybody on the list called Percy," said the nurse.

"He's not a person," Josie Smith said, "he's my panda and the doctor said, I'll whip his tonsils out and it made me have frightening dreams."

"Well, now," said the nurse, "a great girl like you must know the doctor was only joking."

"I do know he was only joking," said Josie Smith, "but he might pretend to take Percy's tonsils out for a joke and if he makes a hole in Percy his stuffing will all come out, my mum said. You have to be careful with him or he'll get spoilt and the doctor doesn't know."

"Well," said the nurse, "you leave him here in bed while you go down to theatre."

"The doctor said I had to bring him. And Eileen's taking her doll down, only the doctor never said he'd take her tonsils out, and anyway she hasn't got stuffing. I don't want him to spoil Percy, I don't want him to touch him. I love him best of anything in the world! I want to take him home!" Josie Smith cried and cried and couldn't stop. The nurse got hold of her hot wet cheeks and said, "You poor little muffin, you have got in a state. Come on. You hold Percy and I'll hold you."

So Josie Smith held Percy's head close to her chest and the nurse held Josie Smith's head close to her chest and rocked them both back and forth.

"Now, then," she said. "You stay like this for a while until you feel better and then you and I'll decide what to do about Percy. Is this what your mum does when you're upset?"

"I sit on her knee," said Josie Smith.

"Ah. It's grand to sit on your mum's knee, but will I do just for tonight?"

Josie Smith nodded. She liked the nice soapy smell of the nurse's uniform and she could feel a little flat watch pinned on the apron, cool against her hot cheek.

"Your name's Josie, isn't it?" whispered the nurse.

"Yes," said Josie Smith.

"And my name's May, like the month of May. Do you like that?"

"Yes," said Josie Smith.

"And do you know what time it is?" said the nurse.

"No," said Josie Smith and she felt for the little watch near her cheek but it was too dark to see.

The nurse shone her torch on it. "It's upside down, do you see that? So I can tell the time from above. It's three o'clock in the morning! And here we are chatting like it was three in the afternoon. I bet you never did that before, did you?"

"No," said Josie Smith, and she giggled.

"Shh! Will you wake every child in the

ward with your giggling! Now, I think you and Percy should settle down for a good sleep while I write a note to the day nurse about Percy. Let me turn your pillow over, it's damp. Down you go. Good girl."

Josie Smith and Percy settled down, and the nurse went back to her desk where the lamp was lit. She wrote a little note and sealed it in an envelope and brought it back to Josie Smith's bed.

"I'll clip it on this board here at the end," she said. "That's where your name and your temperature are written. And

Nurse Bradshaw will find it in the morning. Do you know Nurse Bradshaw? She's grand. She was here when you came in."

"I think I do," said Josie Smith. "She's the one with freckles."

"Hundreds of freckles," said the nurse, "and she'll look after Percy for you while you have your tonsils out. Now you can both go to sleep."

"Can I tell you a secret first?" said Josie Smith in a whisper.

"A secret? I like secrets," said the nurse.

"I have to whisper it in your ear," said Josie Smith.

The nurse came and bent over.

"You won't tell anybody, cross your heart and hope to die?"

"Cross my heart and hope to die," whispered the nurse, "I won't tell. Go on."

"It's a secret about Percy," whispered Josie Smith. "He's not real like a person but if you're not watching him, if you only see him out of the corner of your eye, sometimes he moves. Just a bit."

"He doesn't?" whispered the nurse.

"That's fantastic. And have you told nobody at all except me?"

"I've told my mum," said Josie Smith, "and you. But nobody else."

"And what does your mum say about it?" asked the nurse.

"She says it's because I love him so much," said Josie Smith.

"That's great," the nurse said. "That's a great secret." And she gave Josie Smith a little kiss.

"Goodnight," she said, "and God bless."

And Josie Smith and Percy went to sleep.

The next morning, Josie Smith was sitting up in bed wearing a funny white nightie that fastened down the back, and Eileen was sitting up in her bed wearing just the same. They were both giggling when Nurse Bradshaw came with her trolley.

"What are you two giggling about?" she said.

"We look funny," Josie Smith said, "like babies."

"We've been pretending to cry," Eileen said, "and Josie Smith's been sucking her thumb."

"You're a pair of comics," Nurse Bradshaw said. "Now, here's a little pill for you to take."

"I can't swallow pills," Eileen said. "I only take medicine."

"All right," Nurse Bradshaw said, "you can have the medicine then like the tiny children do." Then she looked at Josie Smith and said, "What about you?"

"I can swallow pills," said Josie Smith with her eyes closed. It wasn't true, but she wanted to be good for Nurse Bradshaw because she was going to look after Percy.

"Here you are, then," Nurse Bradshaw said. "It doesn't taste of anything. Little sip of water. There. Has it gone?"

"Yessh," said Josie Smith with her eyes shut and her mouth shut and the big pill stuck to her tongue.

"Are you sure it's gone down?" Nurse Bradshaw said.

"Yessh," said Josie Smith with her eyes

shut and her mouth shut.

"Open your mouth," Nurse Bradshaw said.

But Josie Smith only opened her eyes and looked worried.

"Not your eyes," Nurse Bradshaw said, "your mouth."

Josie Smith shut her eyes and opened her mouth.

"I thought as much," Nurse Bradshaw said. "Have another little sip of water."

Josie Smith sipped. Then she screwed

up her face and went "Oink!" and swallowed as hard as she could.

"Has it gone down?" Nurse Bradshaw said.

Josie Smith looked worried.

"Oh dear," Nurse Bradshaw said. "Listen, don't try so hard. You're stopping it going down. Just drink some water the same way you always do. Pretend you've got nothing in your mouth. It'll go down by itself."

Josie Smith drank. Then she smiled. "It's gone!" she said, "by itself!"

"Right," Nurse Bradshaw said, "and now Percy's going. Come on, Percy. You can sit in the big chair in the office."

Josie Smith gave Percy a big kiss and a hug and said, "He will be here when I come back, won't he?"

"He'll be here," Nurse Bradshaw said, and she carried Percy away, hugging him with one hand and pushing her trolley with the other.

Eileen said, "I'm taking my doll with me."

Josie Smith didn't say anything.

When Nurse Bradshaw came back with her trolley, Eileen was crying.

"Are you pretending to be a baby again?" Nurse Bradshaw said.

"No," Josie Smith said, "she's not. She's really crying because she says Gary Grimes told her they'd stick great big needles in her in hospital."

"Well, I don't know who Gary Grimes is," Nurse Bradshaw said, "but he must be daft."

"And he said they'd cut her throat with a big knife," Josie Smith said. "He is daft and he's soft as well."

"Knives, is it?" Nurse Bradshaw said. "Well, Gary Grimes doesn't know much about tonsils. They come out like peas out of a pod. Do you need a knife to get peas out of a pod, eh, Eileen? Here you are. Here's some nice syrup instead of the pill."

"I don't want it!" Eileen screamed, "I don't want to have my tonsils out!" and she roared and roared.

"Ah now, that is a shame," Nurse

112

Bradshaw said, "because I've brought this magic cream for your hand. If you're not having your tonsils out I might as well give it all to Josie Smith."

Eileen carried on crying but she was peeping.

"Abracadabra," Nurse Bradshaw said. She rubbed some cream on the back of Josie Smith's hand and winked.

Josie Smith looked at the pot of cream and read the label.

"It doesn't say it's magic," she said, "it says Emla Cream. What does that mean?"

"It really is just like magic," Nurse Bradshaw said, and she stuck a see-through plaster on Josie Smith's hand. "That's so the magic cream doesn't get rubbed off. It's very important and precious. And when you go down to have your tonsils out you'll feel the doctor take hold of your hand with the magic cream on it and before you can count to five you'll be asleep. And the next thing you know you'll be back here in bed with Percy. Well, I'll be off now," and she started pushing her trolley away.

"Mer-her-her!" roared Eileen, "I want some magic cream!"

"Is that right?" said Nurse Bradshaw, "Well, drink your syrup then."

Eileen drank it.

Josie Smith can't remember going down to have her tonsils out or the doctor holding her hand while she fell asleep. Sometimes she says she does remember but she says it with her eyes half closed. She doesn't remember whether she remembers or not because that pill made her feel sleepy.

She slept for a long long time. Once,

she opened her eyes and it was light and people were making a noise. Somebody said, "Josie?" but she was too tired to answer and she went back to sleep. Then she opened her eyes and it was quieter and somebody put a cool hand on her forehead. Josie Smith thought it must be the nice night nurse but she was too tired to look. "Have I had my tonsils out?" she said. Somebody said yes she had.

"Can I have my ice cream now?" she said.

Then she went back to sleep.

After a long time she woke up in the dark and said, "Percy?"

Percy was there next to her. "My throat hurts," she whispered to him.

And she went back to sleep again.

"Wake up, Josie!" said a happy voice. Josie Smith woke up. Nurse Bradshaw was there with Josie Smith's breakfast on a tray. "It's all over. How do you feel?"

Josie Smith sat up and thought about it.

"My throat hurts," she said, "and I don't know what day it is."

"That's because you slept all day yesterday and all night. Today you and Eileen can go home once the doctor's seen you."

Josie Smith and Eileen sat up and ate their breakfast.

"My mum came," Eileen said. "I saw her when I woke up and she brought me some marshmallows because they're soft. And she's coming for me after if the doctor says."

Josie Smith didn't say anything. Her mum had promised she'd be there when she woke up but she wasn't. Josie Smith wondered if her mum knew it was going home day.

After breakfast, Nurse Bradshaw came and washed them and tidied their beds and the doctor came to look at their throats. It wasn't the doctor with the pink face, it was another one. He patted Josie Smith's head and said, "Good girl. You can go home."

Josie Smith wanted to ask him if he'd tell her mum but she didn't say it loud enough and he went to look at Eileen's

throat. He said she could go home, too.

They all put their dressing gowns on and sat at the big table to play with the toys. There was a boy playing dominoes. He stood them on end in a long line like soldiers and then he flicked at the first one with his finger and they all fell down, one by one. A fat little girl held a rabbit in a red coat and watched him. A big boy and girl were playing Snakes and Ladders.

Eileen whispered in Josie Smith's ear, "I know, let's get my doll and your panda and

take them for a walk and look who's in all
the beds." They set off together and read
the names at the ends of the beds.
Sometimes there was somebody in the bed
and sometimes there wasn't. Sometimes the
nurses were changing a bed, waving the big
stiff sheets and tucking them in as fast as
lightning. They saw the little boy who cried
at the other end, only now he was asleep.
Then Eileen ran away, shouting, "My
mum's come!"

Josie Smith looked. Eileen's mum was

coming along the ward with Eileen's clothes in a bag. But there was no Josie's mum with Josie's clothes. Josie Smith's chest went bam bam bam and her face felt hot and frightened. She ran and hid in a corner behind a big trolley full of sheets because she didn't want everybody to know her mum hadn't come. She heard Eileen's mum say, "Where's Josie? I wanted to tell her something." But they didn't find her, and when she peeped out again they'd gone.

Josie Smith came out from behind the trolley and stood in the middle of the room, holding Percy. She didn't know where to go. She thought she would go and sit on her bed, but then she saw Nurse Bradshaw take all the covers and sheets off it so there was only a red rubber sheet left. Then they took the board with her name on it off the end. If her mum didn't come now, where would she sleep? Then she thought of something else.

"My ballet shoes and my book!" She ran to the locker. They were still there, next to her sponge bag. She got them out.

"That's a good girl," said Nurse Bradshaw, pulling a sheet off Eileen's bed. "You get ready for when your mum comes. Just a minute – let me look at you. You're not crying, are you?"

"No," said Josie Smith with her eyes half shut. She wasn't letting any tears squeeze out but she was crying inside her chest and it hurt, like her throat.

"Don't worry," Nurse Bradshaw said. "Your mum'll come and you'll go home, too. I wish you were staying. We're so busy we could do with a helper. Do you think you could push my trolley for me? It's quite heavy."

"I can push the trolley at the supermarket," Josie Smith said, "even if it's full."

"Right. Get pushing, then," Nurse Bradshaw said. "Leave your things inside the locker for now. They'll be all right. And park Percy on top where he can see you."

So Josie Smith pushed the trolley with clean sheets in it and then she pushed a much better trolley with lots of bottles and pills and thermometers on it. She even helped Nurse Bradshaw take some temperatures.

"It's a lucky thing you stayed to help me," Nurse Bradshaw said, "I don't know when we've been so busy. But it's always the same. As soon as I find a good helper they go home."

"I'm not going yet," said Josie Smith, pushing hard at the trolley.

"You are, you know," Nurse Bradshaw said, "or your mum'll have something to say about it. She's just arrived, didn't you notice?"

Josie Smith hadn't noticed. She'd been too busy. But there was her mum coming towards her with Josie Smith's clothes in a bag. Josie Smith didn't run to her right away because she wanted her mum to see her working. She pushed the trolley a bit more and then counted some of the things on it and she could see her mum watching her and smiling.

Then she ran, shouting, "Mum!"

"You look very busy," said Josie's mum, picking her up for a hug.

"We are busy," said Josie Smith. "I don't know when we've been so busy. It's been one of those days. Nurse Bradshaw said."

"But you're going to come home, aren't you?"

"Yes," said Josie Smith, and she forgot her trolley and ran to get Percy and everything from her locker. When her mum was helping her to get dressed she remembered and said, "Why didn't you come like you promised? You weren't there when I woke up."

"Yes she was," Nurse Bradshaw said.

She was putting clean sheets on Eileen's bed.

"You opened your eyes," said Josie's mum, "and you said Have I had my tonsils out? And I said Yes. Don't you remember?"

"I don't think I remember," said Josie Smith.

"And then at teatime you woke up again and you wanted some ice cream."

"I can't remember," said Josie Smith. "I remember somebody's hand, nice and cool."

"My hand," said Josie's mum.

"I thought you hadn't come," said Josie Smith, "and you didn't know I'd had my tonsils out and you didn't come and take me home and Eileen went."

"And didn't Eileen's mum tell you I'd be on the next bus because I had to finish a surprise for you at home?"

"No," said Josie Smith.

"Well, you'll see when we get there. Here, put these on."

"My wellingtons!" shouted Josie Smith.

"Yes," said Josie's mum. "Haven't you looked out of the window? It's been pouring

down all morning. Now, get hold of Percy
and say Goodbye."

Josie Smith got hold of Percy and said
Goodbye.

On the bus she followed the raindrops
trickling down the window and said, "When
I grow up I'm going to be a nurse."

"I'm glad to hear that," said Josie's
mum.

"Why?" said Josie Smith.

"You'll soon see," said Josie's mum.

And she soon saw. She sat on the couch by the front room fire and kept her eyes shut tight until her mum said, "Now you can look."

And she looked.

"A nurse's uniform! It's just like real."

And it was. A stripy blue and white frock with a white collar and little white cuffs on the short sleeves. And an apron and a cap.

"It's hundreds better than Eileen's," Josie Smith said, "because Nurse Bradshaw and Nurse May didn't have a red cross. I'm really going to be a nurse when I grow up."

"And what will Miss Pendlebury say," asked Josie's mum, "if you don't go to dancing class any more?"

"I am going to dancing class," said Josie Smith, "because I'm being a ballet dancer as well. Mum? Can I put my nurse's uniform on now?"

"If you wear your cardigan over it, you can," said Josie's mum, "and keep that rug round you."

So Josie Smith sat on the couch in her nurse's uniform with her cardigan on and the rug round her and Percy on her knee and her ballet shoes on her feet. And she was so happy that she completely forgot that she never did get her ice cream!

Order Form

To order direct from the publishers, just make a list of the titles you want and fill in the form below:

Name ....

Address ....

....

....

Send to: Dept 6, HarperCollins Publishers Ltd, Westerhill Road, Bishopbriggs, Glasgow G64 2QT.

Please enclose a cheque or postal order to the value of the cover price, plus:

UK & BFPO: Add £1.00 for the first book, and 25p per copy for each additional book ordered.

Overseas and Eire: Add £2.95 service charge. Books will be sent by surface mail but quotes for airmail despatch will be given on request.

A 24-hour telephone ordering service is available to holders of Visa, MasterCard, Amex or Switch cards on 0141- 772 2281.

Collins
An *Imprint* of HarperCollins*Publishers*